ELI REMEMBERS

Written by RUTH VANDER ZEE and MARIAN SNEIDER

Illustrated by BILL FARNSWORTH

Eerdmans Books for Young Readers

Grand Rapids, Michigan / Cambridge, U.K.

When I was just a little kid, Great-grandmother Gussie lit seven candles at our family dinner on Rosh Hashanah Eve, sighed, and then whispered a prayer over them.

When Great-grandfather Louis blessed the wine, I watched my great-grandmother. She was still looking at the candles.

A tear fell down her cheek. She wiped it away quickly with her white linen napkin.

I loved being crowded into her small kitchen with my family for the Jewish New Year celebration.

I loved the smell of her roasted chicken, sweet potatoes with fruit, and noodle pudding.

I loved seeing the honey cake on a plate ready for us to eat at the end of the meal. Mom said that just one bite would give us a sweet new year.

"Why does Great-grandmother light seven candles? And why does she cry on such a happy night?" I asked.

My mom leaned over to me. "Eli," she said, "some things are too difficult to talk about."

The year after my great-grandparents died, Grandma Mimi gathered the family at her house for the Rosh Hashanah dinner.

She lit the seven candles and prayed in a strong voice, "May the memory of our family be for a blessing."

Grandpa Sam moved away from the table, the wine, and the candles.

Grandma blessed the wine. I looked into Grandpa's gentle face and saw huge tears in his eyes. They never fell down his cheeks.

"Why is Grandpa sad?" I asked my mom. "Is it a secret?"

"Just like it was with Great-grandmother, Eli. Some things are too difficult to talk about."

I was excited the year my parents invited the family to our house for dinner on Rosh Hashanah Eve.

As Mom was placing the honey cake on the plate, I said, "I hope that Grandpa won't be sad tonight."

We gathered around our dining room table. The smell of roasted chicken filled the room.

Mom lit the seven candles and said, "We light these candles to remember those in our family who are not with us. May their memory be for a blessing."

I couldn't wait for my father to bless the wine. But when he began to speak, he sounded as if he might cry.

I looked around the room.

Again, Grandpa moved away from the table.

My mom's eyes were closed and her hands were pressed together.

Grandma put her hand on my shoulder and hugged me.

Months later, my parents said they would like to take Grandpa and Grandma and me to see the place that Great-grandmother Gussie came from.

We bought tour books, packed our suitcases, and flew to Lithuania.

One of the first things we did there was to find the house where my great-grandmother lived when she was a little girl. We even saw the lake in the center of the village where she swam with her brothers and sisters on summer days.

We shopped in markets, and I met Lithuanian kids. Even though we didn't speak the same language, we played games with the basketball I brought. We danced to folk music and ate food I never heard of. I even learned how to milk a cow.

A few days before we were to return home, my father told me we were going to the Ponar Forest.

"It is a place of remembrance," he said.

Just the way he said it, I knew it must be important.

Mom bought red roses before we left the city. She said that we would take them to honor people who had died.

I sat between Grandpa and Grandma in the van. We traveled a long time. There were no other cars or people along the way.

Finally, I saw a sign that said Ponar Forest.

The van stopped and we climbed out.

It was so quiet!

The only sounds I heard were dogs barking in the distance.

Mom's roses were the only color there.

"It's cold," I shivered.

I climbed up a winding trail, further and further into the forest, crunching the snow with my feet.

I stopped when I came to a wide, deep pit. It had jagged edges. Sharp rocks stuck out through the snow.

It was so quiet now. I couldn't even hear the dogs.

My mom and dad stepped up beside me.

Grandpa and Grandma walked slowly, holding hands, standing back.

"What is this?" I whispered.

Dad spoke quietly. "This is the grave of 80,000 Jews who were killed during World War II. They were force-marched night after night by the Nazis and ordered to stand around this pit. Then the soldiers shot them . . . in their backs . . . "

Dad stood quietly for a long time.

I felt like somebody was hitting my chest.

I waited.

Dad continued, "And then they fell . . .
into this pit. The next day their bodies were
burned."

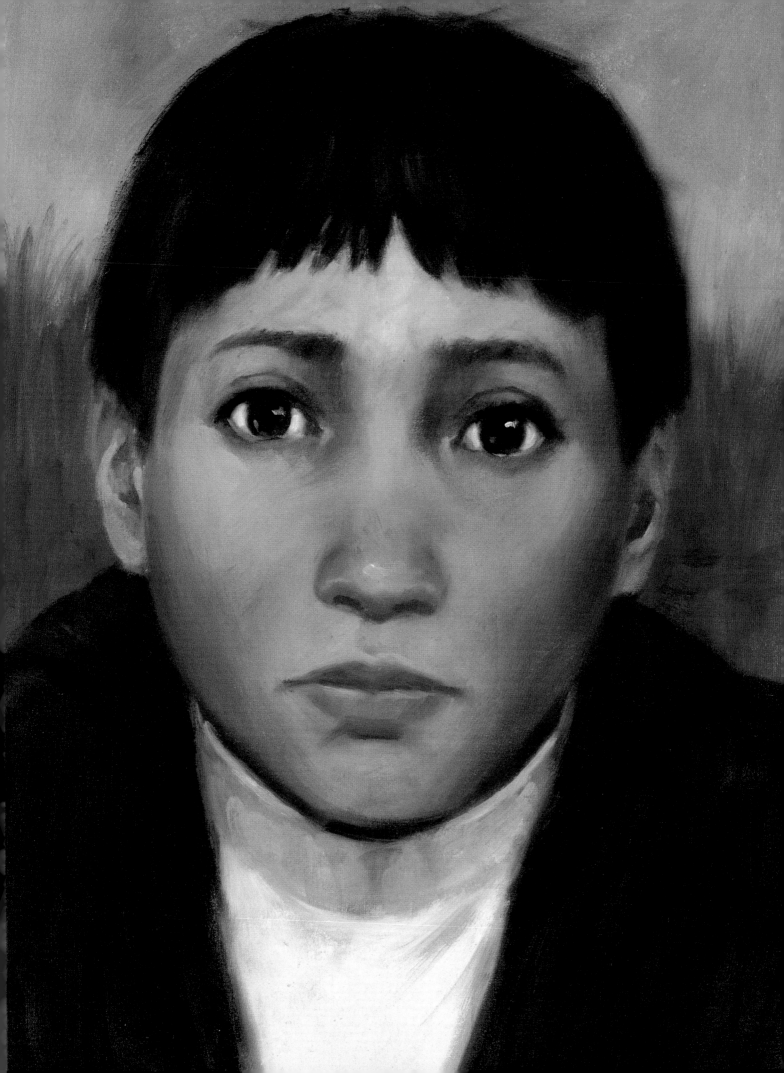

Grandpa moved up and put his arm around me.

"There's more, Eli. Your great-grandmother's father and her six brothers and sisters were killed here. This is their grave."

He took a deep breath.

"Is that why we light seven candles on Rosh Hashanah?" I asked.

"Yes, Eli. That's how we honor their memory."

He paused. "Once, when I was about your age, I asked my mother about her father and brothers and sisters. But she cried so much when she told me . . . " Grandpa's voice got quiet. "None of our family ever talks about what happened here."

We stood looking into the pit for a long time.

"Were children killed too?"

"Yes," Grandpa said.

"My age?"

"Yes, your age and younger."

I felt as gray as the sky.

I walked to my mom, took seven roses from her bouquet, and climbed down to the center of the pit.

I made a small mound of snow and arranged the roses on it. Just like Great-grandmother Gussie's seven candles.

Then I stood on the graves of our family, raised my hands, and said the familiar prayer I learned many years ago.

"Hear, O Israel, the Lord our God, the Lord is One."

I looked up at my grandpa. Tears were rolling down his face.

He held out his arms to me.

I climbed up out of the pit and went to him.

"It's okay, Grandpa," I said. "It won't be a secret anymore. I'll always remember."

AUTHOR'S NOTE

The Ponar Forest is a thickly wooded place located six miles from the capital city of Vilnius, Lithuania. In 1941 the Soviet government dug large pits in this forest to be used as storage for fuel tanks. When the Nazis occupied Lithuania during World War II, they began using the Ponar Forest as a killing field, and the pits became graves for between 70,000 and 100,000 people, mostly Jews.

In this story, when Eli sees the pits and learns that his ancestors were among the executed Jews, he finally understands why sadness is part of his family's observance of Rosh Hashanah. Traditionally, this holiday is a time when Jews celebrate and look forward to the coming year. The prayer Eli recites at the execution pit is called the Sh'ma, the central prayer of the Jewish faith.

This book is based on actual events, inspired by coauthor Marian Sneider's grandson Ely Sandler. This story was also the subject of a British television documentary, which first aired in May 2004.

— Ruth Vander Zee

For my mom, Minnie Dykstra
— *R. V. Z.*

For Stanley
— *M. S.*

For Hodge
— *B. F.*

ও   ৬

This book is dedicated in loving memory to Marian Sneider by her family.
Sadly, Marian passed away in December 2005, before the book's publication.

ও   ৬

Text © 2007 Ruth Vander Zee and Marian Sneider
Illustrations © 2007 Bill Farnsworth

Published in 2007 by Eerdmans Books for Young Readers,
an imprint of Wm. B. Eerdmans Publishing Co.

Wm. B. Eerdmans Publishing Co.
2140 Oak Industrial Dr. NE, Grand Rapids, Michigan 49505
P.O. Box 163, Cambridge CB3 9PU U.K.

www.eerdmans.com/youngreaders

Manufactured in United States of America

07 08 09 10 11   8 7 6 5 4 3 2 1

Library of Congress Cataloging-in-Publication Data

Vander Zee, Ruth.
Eli remembers / written by Ruth Vander Zee and Marian Sneider;
illustrated by Bill Farnsworth.
p. cm.
Summary: After many years of watching the solemn lighting of
seven candles at Rosh Hashanah, Eli finally learns how those candles
represent his family's connection to the Holocaust in Lithuania.
ISBN 978-0-8028-5309-7 (hardcover : alk. paper)
[1. Jews — United States — Fiction. 2. Rosh ha-Shanah — Fiction.
3. Family — Fiction. 4. Holocaust, Jewish (1939-1945) — Lithuania
— Fiction.] I. Sneider, Marian. II. Farnsworth, Bill, ill. III. Title.
PZ7.V285116Eli 2007
[Fic] — dc22
                                    2006026513

Illustrations created with oils on canvas
Display type set in Trajan Pro
Text type set in Weiss
Gayle Brown, Art Director